The Big Baby Bear Book

John Prater

TED SMART

To Melissa

This edition is produced for The Book People Ltd,
Hall Wood Avenue, Haydock, St Helens WA11 9 UL

Copyright © John Prater 2001

Number One, Tickle Your Tum, first published by The Bodley Head, © John Prater 1999
The Bear Went Over the Mountain, first published by The Bodley Head, © John Prater 1999
Oh Where, Oh Where? first published by The Bodley Head, © John Prater 1998
Walking Round the Garden, first published by The Bodley Head, © John Prater 1998

The author wishes to acknowledge Ivan Hicks at *The Garden In Mind,* Stanstead House, West Sussex

1 3 5 7 9 10 8 6 4 2

The right of John Prater to be identified as the author and illustrator of this work
has been asserted by him in accordance with the Copyright, Designs and Patents Act, 1988.

First published in Great Britain in 2001 by
The Bodley Head Children's Books
An imprint of The Random House Group Limited
20 Vauxhall Bridge Road, London, SW1V 2SA

Random House Australia (Pty) Ltd
20 Alfred Street, Milsons Point, Sydney
New South Wales 2061, Australia

Random House New Zealand Limited
18 Poland Road, Auckland 10, New Zealand

Random House South Africa (Pty) Ltd
Endulini, 5A Jubilee Road,
Parktown 2193, South Africa

Printed in Singapore by Tien Wah Press (Pte) Ltd

A CIP catalogue record for this book is available from the British Library

THE RANDOM HOUSE GROUP Limited Reg. No. 954009

www.randomhouse.co.uk

Contents

Grandbear and Me 9

Rumbling Tummies 31

Me and My Friends 45

Out and About 57

Bedtime 77

Grandbear
and Me

Number One, Tickle Your Tum

Shall we play the counting game?

Number one tickle your tum.

Number two just say, 'BOO!'

Number three touch your knee.

Number four touch the floor.

Number five do a dive.

Number six wiggle your hips.

Number seven jump to heaven.

Number eight stand up straight.

Number nine walk in line.

Number ten start again.

What a clever little bear!

We can play on the little flute,
And this is the music to it:

Tootle toot toot
  goes the little flute,

Meeny minn minn
  goes the violin,

Ruma tum tum
  goes the kettle drum,

Plom plom plom
goes the old banjo,

Ticka ticka teck
go the castanets,

Jing a ting ting
goes the tambourine,

Zoom, zoom, zoom
goes the double bass,

Rum, boom, boom

goes the big bass drum,

Ta, ta, tara

goes the bugle horn,
And this is the way to do it!

The boughs do shake
And the bells do ring,
So merrily comes our harvest in,
Our harvest in, our harvest in.

We've ploughed, we've sowed,
We've reaped,
We've mowed,
We've got our harvest in.

To market, to market
to buy a fat pig,
Home again, home again,
jiggetty-jig.

The Bear Went Over the Mountain

The bear went over the mountain...

The bear went over the mountain...

The bear went over the mountain...

To see what he could see.

And the other side of the mountain...

The other side of the mountain...

The other side of the mountain...

Was all that he could see.

So he went back over the mountain...

He went back over the mountain...

He went back over the mountain...

So very happily.

Tickly tickly
On your knee,
If you laugh,
You don't love me.

Hickory Dickory Dock,
The mouse ran up the clock;
The clock struck one,
The mouse ran down,
Hickory Dickory Dock!

As I looked out on
    Saturday last
A fat little bear
    went hurrying past.

I waved at him,
    but he didn't see
For he never so much
    as looked at me.

Once again
    when the moon was high
I saw the little bear
    hurrying by.

And he smiled with a face
    that was quite content
But I never found out
    where that little bear went.

Rumbling Tummies

If all the world was paper
And all the sea was ink
If all the trees were bread and cheese
What should we have to drink?

One, two, three, four
Bunny's at the cottage door.
Five, six, seven, eight
Eating cherries off a plate.

Oh Where, Oh Where?

Oh where, oh where has my little bear gone?

Oh where, oh where can he be?

With his soft little paws, and big wet nose,

Oh where, oh where is he?

Oh where, oh where has my little bear gone?

Oh where, oh where can he be?

With his waggly ears, and twinkly eyes,

Oh where, oh where is he?

Oh there, oh there is my dear little bear.

Come over here to me.

A kiss and a cuddle I need from you,

Before we have our tea.

Five currant buns in
   a baker's shop,
Round and sweet
   with a cherry on the top.

Along came a bear
   with a penny one day,
Bought a currant bun
   and took it away.

I'm a little teapot,
   short and stout;
Here's my handle,
   here's my spout.

When I get the
   steam up,
Hear me shout,

'Tip me up
   and pour me out.'

Algy met a bear
A bear met Algy
The bear was bulgy
The bulge was Algy.

Me and My Friends

The bears on the bus
Go hip-hooray,
Hip-hooray,
Hip-hooray,
The bears on the bus
Go hip-hooray,
All day long.

The bell on the bus
Goes ding-a-ling-ling,
Ding-a-ling-ling,
Ding-a-ling-ling,
The bell on the bus
Goes ding-a-ling-ling,
All day long.

The wipers on the bus
Go swish-swish-swish,
Swish-swish-swish,
Swish-swish-swish,
The wipers on the bus
Go swish-swish-swish,
All day long.

Miss Polly had a dolly
who was
sick, sick, sick.

So she phoned for
the doctor to come
quick, quick, quick.

The doctor came
with his bag and his hat,
And he knocked
on the door
with a rat-a-tat-tat.

He looked at the dolly,
  and he shook his head,
And he said, 'Miss Polly,
  put her straight to bed'.

He wrote on
  a paper for a
  pill, pill, pill.

'I'll be back
  in the morning
  with my
  bill, bill, bill.'

Humpty Dumpty
sat on a wall,
Humpty Dumpty
had a great fall.
All the King's horses and
all the King's men
couldn't put Humpty
together again.

My little house won't stand up straight,
My little house has lost its gate,
My little house bends up and down,
My little house is the oldest in town.

Here comes the wind,
It blows and blows again,
Down falls my little house.
Oh, what a shame!

Ring-a-ring o' roses,
A pocket full of posies,
A-tish-oo, a-tish-oo,
We all fall down!

The robin on the steeple,
Is singing to the people,
A-tish-oo, a-tish-oo,
We all stand up!

Down at the station, early in the morning,
see the little puffer-billies all in a row.

See the engine driver pull his little lever,
Puff, puff, peep, peep, off we go!

Heads, shoulders, knees and toes, knees and toes,
Heads, shoulders, knees and toes, knees and toes,

And eyes and ears, and mouth and nose,

Heads, shoulders, knees and toes, knees and toes.

Out and About

Row, row, row your boat,
Gently down the stream;
Merrily, merrily,
Merrily, merrily,
Life is but a dream.

Hush–a–bye, baby,
On the tree top,
When the wind blows,
The cradle will rock;
When the bough breaks,
The cradle will fall,
And down will come baby,
Cradle and all.

I hear thunder,
I hear thunder;
Hark, don't you?
Hark, don't you?

Pitter-patter raindrops,
Pitter-patter raindrops,
I'm wet through,
So are you.

One, two,
   kittens that mew,

Two, three,
   birds in a tree,

Three, four,
   shells on a shore,

Four, five,
   bees from a hive,

Five, six,
   the cow that licks,

Six, seven,
  stars in the heaven.

Seven, eight,
  sheep at the gate,

Eight, nine,
  swing on the vine,

Nine, ten,
  the little black hen.

Winter has passed, and Spring is here,
With longer days, and warming sun,
There are seeds to be sown,
  and clippings to clear,
So much to do, now Spring has sprung.

Time for bed?
That can't be right.
Time for bed?
But it's still light.
Time for bed?
Keep still and hide,
We'd rather play
Than go inside.

Autumn leaves come tumbling down,
Yellow, orange, red and brown.
Kick them, scatter them, throw them around,
As Grandbear tries to clear the ground.

The north wind does blow
And we shall have snow,
So blow, North Wind, blow,
And bring us more snow.

73

How do you like to go up in a swing
   up in the air so blue?
Oh I do think it is the pleasantest thing
   ever a bear can do.
Up in the air and over the wall
   till I can see so wide
Rivers and trees and cattle and all
   over the countryside
Till I look down on the garden green
   down on the roof so brown
Up in the air I go flying again
   up in the air and down.

R. L. Stevenson

Rain on the green grass
And rain on the tree
Rain on the housetop
But not on me.

Here I am
Little Jumping Joan
When nobody's with me,
I'm all alone.

Bedtime

There were five in the bed
And the little one said,
'Roll over.'
So they all rolled over
and one fell out.

There were four in the bed
And the little one said,
'Roll over.'
So they all rolled over
and one fell out.

There were three in the bed
And the little one said,
'Roll over.'
So they all rolled over
and one fell out.

There were two in the bed
And the little one said,
'Roll over.'
So they all rolled over
and one fell out.

And the little one said,
'Oooh, that's better.'

Walking Round the Garden

Walking round the garden,

like a teddy bear,

One step, two steps,

tickle you under there.

THE BIG BABY BEAR BOOK

Walking down the hallway,

up and up the stairs,

One step, two steps,

what a clever bear!

Sitting in the bedroom,

what a sleepy ted,

All I need is a goodnight kiss,

then tuck you into bed.

Twinkle, twinkle, little star,
How I wonder what you are!
Up above the world so high,
Like a diamond in the sky,
Twinkle, twinkle, little star,
How I wonder what you are!

Star light, star bright
First star I see tonight.
I wish I may, I wish I might
Have the wish I wish tonight.

I see the moon,
The moon sees me.
God bless the moon
And God bless me.

Golden slumbers
Kiss your eyes,
Smiles await you
When you rise.
Sleep, little baby,
Don't you cry,
And I will sing
A lullaby.